Cheesemares

Ross Collins

First published in 2013 in Great Britain by
Barrington Stoke Ltd
18 Walker Street, Edinburgh, EH3 7LP

www.barringtonstoke.co.uk

ISBN: 978-1-78112-191-7

Printed in China by Leo

This book has dyslexia-friendly features

For Patricia, Gregor and Bran

Contents

Chapter 1:
Aaaaaaah!

Chapter 2:
Another Cheesemare

"Was it another bad dream?" asked Hal's mum. "A nightmare?" asked Hal's dad with a yawn.

"No," said Hal. He picked up his pad and pencil. "It was another **cheesemare**."

"You will just have to stop eating cheese before bed!" snapped Hal's dad as he and Hal's mum stumbled back to their room. "You're becoming obsessed!"

It was true. Hal had been sure for weeks that there must be a link between his cheesy snacks and the nightmares he kept having.

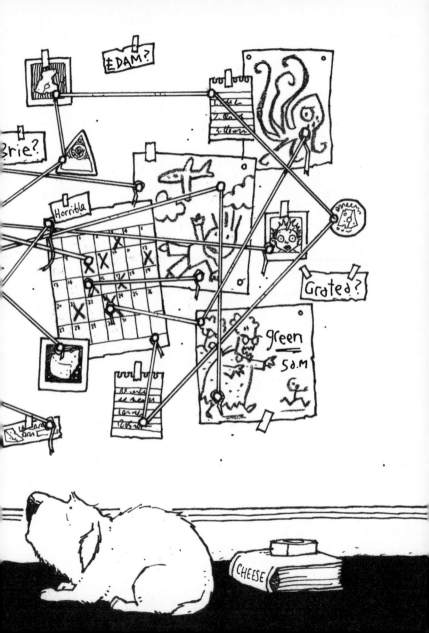

Hal first spotted the link the night he ate some smelly French cheese and had a horrible dream about vampires with poisonous cowboy boots.

He began to try different cheeses to find out what happened. Edam gave him nightmares of pork pies with teeth

hiding in the u-bend of the loo. Danish Blue cheese woke Hal with a start from a dream of great big green grannies. Cheddar made him dream of kittens with 16 eyes. Gorgonzola made him see electric newsreaders with skin-melting farts. Hal tried to forget what he saw after a few small bites of Stilton.

Hal sat down with a thump in front of his Cheesemares Wall.

"This can't go on," he said to Rufus (who wasn't really listening). **"Tomorrow I'm going to solve the Case of the Cheesemares once and for all."**

"Today I'm going to solve the Case of the Cheesemares once and for all," Hal said to his mum as he scoffed down his bran flakes.

Chapter 3:
Where to Start?

"That's nice, dear," said Hal's mum, and patted his head.

Hal figured that it could take a while to solve the Case of the Cheesemares. He packed some snacks in his pocket, pulled on some sturdy boots and took a jumper in case it got chilly. He packed his case files into a backpack and went downstairs.

His mum stood at the front door.
She had Hal's Captain Calamity lunch
box and Rufus' lead in her hands.

"Here's some lunch in case you get
hungry," she said.

"And take Rufus. He's fat and needs more walks."

Once Hal was outside he wasn't too sure where to start. He took one of the labels he had collected from the different cheeses, out of his backpack.

"Where to start ... where to start ...?" he said to himself.

"Shop," growled Rufus.

"I know!" said Hal. "We'll start at the cheese shop!"

Chapter 4:
The Trail

Hal tied Rufus up outside the cheese shop. Most of the time Rufus wasn't happy about not being allowed into shops but he didn't mind with the cheese shop.

The smell was horrific.

Hal took one last gasp of fresh air and went in.

"Good morning, Mr Halloumi," said Hal.

"Good morning, Hal," smiled Mr Halloumi.

Mr Halloumi had seen a lot of Hal over the last month.

"And what cheese can I tempt you with today, my friend?" asked Mr Halloumi as he wiped some Feta off his apron.

"No cheese today," said Hal. "I need to solve the Case of the Cheesemares."

He handed a pile of labels from his backpack to Mr Halloumi. "All of these cheeses give me terrible nightmares and I want to find out why."

"Oh dear," said Mr Halloumi. "That's no good at all. Let me have a look at these." He shuffled through the labels then went off to the back shop. Hal sniffed some Stilton while he waited.

After a while Mr Halloumi came back through.

"I'm sorry. I can't solve the Case of the Cheesemares for you, Hal," he said. "But I can tell you one thing – all these cheeses came from the same factory." He held out an order form which said:

Contessa Von Udderstein's
(not-at-all-evil)
House of Cheese
Lovely Cheeses for the Kiddies

"This could be the lead I'm after," said Hal as he untied Rufus' lead. "But where do we go next?"

"Airport," said Rufus.

Chapter 5:
Getting There

"Two tickets for Bovinia, please," said Hal to a lady at the airport.

"You're in luck," said the lady, whose make-up made her head look huge. "We've got a deal on flights to Bovinia today – Mucho Cheapo!"

"Sorry?" said Hal

"They're cheap," said the lady. "60p for you, 70p for the dog."

"Why is Rufus' ticket more than mine?" asked Hal.

"Because he's fat and we'll have to hoover the seat after."

Rufus scowled at the lady.

The flight didn't take long at all.
There were magazines, snacks and a
film about a lobster that went into outer
space.

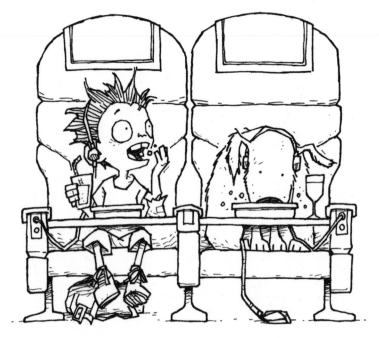

When Hal showed the address to a lady in the airport she told him where the train station was.

The train was very busy. There were magazines and snacks but no film.

Then Hal and Rufus had to get a bus.
There were magazines but no snacks or
film.

After that, Hal and Rufus travelled by goat. There were no magazines, snacks or film.

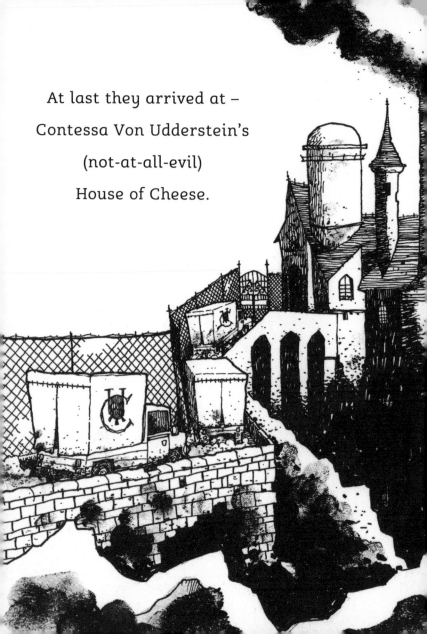

At last they arrived at –
Contessa Von Udderstein's
(not-at-all-evil)
House of Cheese.

Chapter 6:
The House of Cheese

"Contessa von Udderstein's Not-at-all-Evil House of Cheese doesn't look very not-at-all-evil to me," said Hal.

It was true. Hal and Rufus hid behind some rocks and watched as grubby trucks with dark windows drove in and out of the House of Cheese.

It was huge. Half-factory, half-castle. Three massive chimneys belched muddy green smoke into the air above.

Now and then a bird would fly too close to the smoke, choke, and drop from the sky like a stone. The smell was terrible – even worse than the smell of Mr Halloumi's shop back at home.

"Well, we can't tell much from here, Rufus," said Hal. "Let's get inside and have a closer look."

Rufus didn't look too keen.

Hal and Rufus climbed down the rocks. They took care not to be seen by the trucks as they drove to and from the House of Cheese.

The trucks had to wait in a line to enter the factory. Hal and Rufus ran up to the last truck and jumped into the back. They pulled the cover over once they were in. The old truck started up and they heard a buzzer screech as it was let in to the House of Cheese.

Hal and Rufus watched through a crack in the side of the truck.

When no one was looking they jumped out and ran deeper into the factory.

"Let's head upstairs to get a good view," hissed Hal. He ran off up some shaky old steps and Rufus wheezed along behind him.

Going upstairs may not have been the best idea. It gave them a great view of the House of Cheese but the smell and fumes got worse as they climbed.

Rufus' poor doggy nose started to turn purple. Hal took a hanky from his pocket and poked it up Rufus' nostrils.

That took care of the smell, but by then the fumes were making Hal's eyes stream with tears. He rubbed them and blinked down at the factory floor. It must be the tears, he couldn't quite see, for a moment it looked like ... it couldn't be ... it looked like ...

"The House of Cheese is run by COWS!" gasped Hal.

Chapter 7:
Aaaaachoooo!

Hal couldn't believe his eyes.

Hundreds of cows were busy down on the factory floor, some wore grubby white coats, others were in grubby

overalls. They walked around on
their back legs, looking after the ugly
machines, packing the cheese, and
driving little forklift trucks around. It
didn't seem possible.

Hal turned to Rufus to check it wasn't all a dream. Rufus wasn't too bothered about the cows – he was more bothered by the hanky up his nose.

His left nostril **twitched**.

Hal gasped.

His right nostril **itched**.

"No, Rufus! No!" hissed Hal

His nose

wiggled ... jiggled ... **wriggled** ...

and ...

Rufus felt better after that. Hal didn't. The busy factory had just become very very still ... apart from the sound of hooves ... **getting closer**.

In a moment the patrol cows were on them.

"A HOOMAN!" mooed one, as it grabbed Hal.

"**AND A FAT DOG!**" mooed another as it grabbed Rufus.

Rufus decided he didn't like cows.

Other patrol cows soon arrived. There was no chance of escape.

"**Take them to ...**

CONTESSA VON UDDERSTEIN!"

Chapter 8:
The Contessa

The cow patrol dragged Hal and Rufus down corridor after corridor, deep into the House of Cheese. Hal tried every trick he knew to get away. But every time he slowed down or pretended to tie his shoelace one of the patrol cows would push his back with a sharp hoof and shout, "**MOOOOVE!**"

Soon they came to a grand doorway. One of the patrol cows stepped forward and rang the little cowbell that hung from the frame.

"Moo is it?" came a shrill voice from inside.

"It's the patrol cows!" called the patrol cow.

"We've arrested a hooman and a fat dog!"

"Just a mooment!" called the voice. There was a sound of dainty hoof-steps and then the voice bellowed, "**COME!**"

Hal and Rufus were pushed into a room which would have made Kings and Queens feel a bit poor. In the middle of that room stood the most evil cow in the world. **The Contessa von Udderstein.**

"So!" hissed the Contessa. "Hooman spies, is it? The last hoomans that sneaked in here were **cooked alive** in moolted cheese!"

Hal gulped. "You don't scare me, von Udderstein!" he yelled.

"Oh ... but I think I moo!" mocked the Contessa. "I scare millions of little hooman children like you **EVERY NIGHT** with my **CHEESEMARES!**"

"So it's true!" gasped Hal. "Your cheese does give children cheesemares! But why?"

"**Why**? **Why**?!" snapped the Contessa. "Like you don't know! **THEFT**! That's why! **Theft**! For years you nasty little hoomans have been **STEALING OUR MILK**! Stealing it with your little hooman fingers on your little hooman hands. **Stealing it!** And for what? To make milk shakes and yoghurt and ice cream and cheese and butter and sour cream and fudge and curds and whey and lassi and custard and ..."

"I get the picture," said Hal

"**Yes**! I'm sure you moo!" snapped the Contessa. "And soon billions of children across the world will get the picture too! They'll get horrible pictures in their nasty little heads EVERY NIGHT! EVERYWHERE! We're going GLOBAL! Evil cheese made with our evil milk will soon be rolled out ... around the WORLD!"

The Contessa began to laugh. It was not a nice laugh.

It was a horrible evil cow laugh.

"Moo Hoo Ha! MOO! HOO HOO HA!"

Rufus decided he liked evil cow laughter even less than having a hanky up his nose.

"Run," he said.

"What?" said Hal

"**Run!**" barked Rufus. He jumped up and bit Contessa von Udderstein right on the udder.

Chapter 9:
Run!

There isn't another sound on earth that is as awful as the scream of an evil cow that has a fat dog biting her udder.

Contessa von Udderstein was a very mad cow. She thrashed this way and that in an attempt to throw off Rufus as evil milk spurted around the room.

The patrol cows ran to and fro, trying to grab Rufus as he was swung around and around. None of them could catch him. Any that did, found that hooves couldn't hold onto flying fur for very long.

Hal watched for a moment before he remembered Rufus' advice and ran!

Hal fled up and down many corridors before he found himself in the main hall on the factory floor. The cow patrol upstairs must have noticed that he had gone, as alarm bells began to ring around the House of Cheese. Red lights flashed on the walls, and lit up the horrific machines.

Hal could hear hooves hammer the floor as the cows spread out to track him down.

It wasn't long before they found him.

"**Here's the hooman!**" a voice shouted. "**Get it!**" mooed another.

Hal leapt from the grasp of one cow, almost into the hooves of another.

He was smaller and faster than they were but there were lots of them and they were closing in. Hal reckoned he should head up the way, in the hope that the cows weren't good climbers.

Hal jumped up onto a huge mixing machine and began to climb.

The cows followed. They were surprisingly nimble. Hal leapt from the mixing machine onto one with big paddles. Still the cows followed.

They were getting closer.

Hal ran along the top, grabbed a long tube and swung across to a vast cooling tank.

There was a ladder on the side of the tank, and Hal began to climb. He looked down. The cows weren't very good at swinging but they would find a way across soon.

Hal climbed on, higher and higher until he reached the top. He looked down the other side to see the cows on the way up. He looked back the way he had come. More cows were making their way up the ladder. **He was trapped!**

Hal sat down on the top of the tank. There was a flap open next to him and he could see evil green milk churning inside the tank. It swirled and splashed around and the horrid smell rose up to meet Hal's nostrils.

Hal pulled away and began to search in his backpack. Did he have anything that could help him escape?

A sandwich? No.

A biscuit? No.

'Goat Farming Today' magazine? No.

A carton of 'Happy Dairies Pure Milk'? ...

'What would happen,' thought Hal, 'to an **evil milk machine** if some **pure milk** was poured into it?'

There was only one way to find out.
Hal popped off the cap and poured the
clean white milk into the churning green
below.

For a moment nothing happened.

Then there was a **creak**.

Then a **deep groan** inside the tank.

The cows stopped climbing.

A small puff of steam hissed out of the machine.

Then the **bangs** started and the **clunks** and the **clanks**.

The cows ran.

They didn't care about Hal any more. They just ran for it, some on two legs, some on four for even more speed.

Hal thought running for it might be a good idea.

He slid down the side of the machine and ran as fast as he could towards the daylight.

He ran as fast as his legs would carry him out of the House of Cheese.

He ran fast, but not as fast as Rufus, who appeared next to him, with what looked like the end of a cow tail in his mouth.

They just managed to get to a safe distance before they turned to see …

Chapter 10:
Getting Back

Chapter 11:
Case Closed

Hal and Rufus made it home just in time for tea.

"Well?" asked Hal's mum

"Did you solve the Case of the Cheesemares once and for all?"

"Yes, thank you," said Hal

"That's nice," said Hal's mum. "You're just in time for dinner. Go and wash your hands."

"You're in luck, son," smiled Hal's dad. "It's your favourite. Macaroni cheese."

Our books are tested
for children and young people by
children and young people.

Thanks to everyone who consulted on
a manuscript for their time and effort in
helping us to make our books better
for our readers.